# VAMPIRE ACROSS THE WAY

Benjy thinks his mysterious neighbour might be a vampire – but if he isn't, what is he?

Dyan Sheldon is a children's writer, adult novelist and humorist. Her titles for younger children include *Elena the Frog*, *He's Not My Dog*, *Leon Loves Bugs*, and the Lizzie and Charley series, as well as *Undercover Angel* and *Undercover Angel Strikes Again*. Among her numerous titles for young adults are *Confessions of a Teenage Drama Queen* – now a major feature film starring Lindsay Lohan and Adam Garcia – and its sequel, *My Perfect Life*; *Sophie Pitt-Turnbull Discovers America*; *The Boy of My Dreams*; *Tall Thin and Blonde*; *Planet Janet* and its sequel *Planet Janet in Orbit*. American by birth, Dyan Sheldon lives in north London.

Books by the same author

*Elena the Frog*
*He's Not My Dog*
*Leon Loves Bugs*
*Lizzie and Charley Go Shopping*
*Lizzie and Charley Go to the Movies*
*Lizzie and Charley Go Away for the Weekend*

# DYAN SHELDON

Illustrations by Tony Ross

WALKER BOOKS

AND SUBSIDIARIES

LONDON • BOSTON • SYDNEY • AUCKLAND

First published 2004 by Walker Books Ltd
87 Vauxhall Walk, London SE11 5HJ

2 4 6 8 10 9 7 5 3 1

Text © 2004 Dyan Sheldon
Illustrations © 2004 Tony Ross

This book has been typeset in Garamond

Printed in Great Britain by J.H. Haynes & Co. Ltd

British Library Cataloguing in Publication Data:
a catalogue record for this book
is available from the British Library

ISBN 0-7445-6146-9

www.walkerbooks.co.uk

# Contents

# The New Neighbours

My best mate Cas and I were
watching a horror film when my
brother Dean called us. He was
peering through the curtains of the
front window like a spaceship had
just landed in our road.

"What is it?" I asked.

"We've got new neighbours."

Cas and I jumped up. The house across the road was the only other house for miles. New neighbours were even more interesting than an alien invasion.

Cas and I squeezed in beside Dean. A large removals van was in the drive and all the lights were on.

"It's weird," said Dean. "Nobody moves house at night."

"Maybe they got caught in traffic," said Cas.

The removal men lifted a long wooden crate from the van.

I leant closer to the window. "What's that?"

"It looks like a coffin," said Dean.

"Don't be daft." I gave him a poke. "Nobody keeps a cof—"

A large black car with tinted windows turned into the drive and stopped beside the van. Only one person got out. We could tell it was a man, but he was wearing a wide-brimmed hat and had his collar up so we couldn't see his face.

"Jeez," said Cas. "D'you think that's your new neighbour?"

"No," said Dean, "it's the bloke to read the meter."

# The Invisible Man

"It's the oddest thing," Mum said one night, "but no one has met our new neighbour yet. Not even Mrs Pottle." Mrs Pottle was our postman. "Still, I suppose if he's at work all day…"

"But he's not. His car's always in the drive." I'd been watching. "Except at night. That's the only time it's ever gone."

Mum gave me a look. "I hope you're not spying on our neighbour, Benjy."

"Course not." I picked up my fork. "But it is odd."

"I'm sure there's a logical explanation," said Mum.

I wasn't so sure. "Well, I think it's weird. A month's a long time."

"Ooooh!" shrieked Dean. "A mystery!" He leant back in his chair. "He could be a criminal … or a terrorist—"

"That's enough Dean." Mum had on her no-nonsense face. "I don't suppose it's occurred to either of you that the poor man may have to work at night and sleep during the day?"

Dean grinned. "I know! Our new neighbour's a vampire."

"Wow," I said. "A vampire!" I couldn't wait to tell Cas. Neither of us had thought of that.

"You know vampires aren't real, Benjy." Now it was me Mum was glaring at. "Don't start getting carried away by your imagination."

"I won't," I said.

But that wasn't true.

# My Life as a Spy

I spied on our neighbour from my window whenever I could.

But I never saw anyone.

And then Dean caught me rummaging in the hall cupboard.

"What are you up to, Benjy?"

"Me?" I shrugged. "Nothing."

"That's not Mum's binoculars you've got there, is it?"

I tried to hide them. "Course not. What would I be doing with them?"

"You know," Dean shook his head sadly, "it always ends badly when you try to be a hero. Remember last time."

The last time was when I tried to rescue a cat from the big conker tree. The cat got down on its own, but I couldn't. There was a photo of me being carried down by a fireman in the local paper. Dean had it in a frame over his desk.

"And vampires are more dangerous than cats," said Dean.

"Vampires?" I spluttered with laughter. "There's no such thing as vampires!"

"Course not," said Dean.

But he didn't say it like he meant it. He said it like I was a little kid who had to be lied to.

"Then I reckon you can put the binoculars back – since you don't need them."

"Right," I said, "I'll put them away."

But if I could prove the bloke across the road was a vampire I'd be sure to get my picture in the paper again. And this time it would be one *I* could frame and hang over *my* desk.

# Two Heroes
# for the Price of One

The binoculars didn't help. I still never saw anyone come or go, and I still couldn't see inside the house because the curtains were always closed. Which was what you'd expect from a vampire. Criminals and terrorists aren't afraid of the sun.

Then one night Cas slept over.
This was our chance. With Cas
there to keep me awake we could
watch all night long.

But by midnight I was getting
sleepy.

"I don't know how much longer
I can hold out," I admitted.

"Me neither." Cas rubbed his eyes.
"I think I just saw that bush at the
side of the house move."

I yawned.

Cas said, "There! It moved again!"

I lifted the
binoculars.
"That's not the
bush moving.
That's something
with legs."

It was our strange neighbour.
I recognized his hat. One minute
he was beside the bush, and the
next he was driving away.

"Off to find his next victim," said
Cas.

"Come on," I said, "let's go."

"Go where?" asked Cas.

"Across the road."

Cas blinked. "What for?"

"I reckon the door to the cellar's behind that bush."

"Are you mad?" demanded Cas.

"I just want to see if he left it open."

"And what if he did?"

I sighed. "Then we'll see if his coffin's down there."

"I don't want to see if his coffin's down there," said Cas.

"Why not? If he is a vampire he won't be back till dawn."

Cas didn't say anything.

"And if he really is a vampire, we have to prove it, don't we?" I put an arm round his shoulder. "Think of it, Cas. We'll be heroes."

# Cas and I Enter
# the Vampire's Cave

You don't just march into a
vampire's cellar unprepared.

"We need a crucifix," I decided.

"And where are we going to get
that?" asked Cas.

"We can make one." I grabbed
two pencils and an elastic band
from my desk. "What d'you think?"

Cas frowned. "It looks like two pencils tied together with an elastic band."

"But in the shape of a cross."

"Maybe we should take a mirror, too," Cas suggested. "They don't like mirrors."

"Forget it. The only mirror small enough to carry is in the budgie's cage."

"What about garlic?"

My mum bought garlic in a jar.
I didn't reckon waving a jar about
was going to have much effect.

"We don't need garlic either. The
cross should be enough."

Cas was still frowning. "We do
need a torch."

I had a small torch in my desk.
I turned it on.

"It's pathetic," said Cas.

"It'll have to do."

Silently, we tiptoed
downstairs, out the
front door and into
the night.

"If there is a cellar door it's probably locked," Cas whispered.

I almost hoped he was right.

The cellar door was in the ground where I'd thought it would be. I shone my torch on it.

"What did I tell you?" There was only a bar keeping it shut. "And it's not locked." I removed the bar and pulled.

All we could see was the top step.

"Benjy…" said Cas.

"You're not chickening out on me, are you?"

Cas raised his chin. "Course not."

That was lucky. I didn't fancy going down there on my own.

Cas gripped my arm as we walked down the steps. "I don't like this, Benjy."

That was when the door banged shut.

"It's just the wind," I whispered.

A new noise made us jump again.

Cas's fingers tightened on my arm. "Is that the wind, too?"

It didn't sound like it. It sounded like the bar being slipped back into place.

Desperation got us back up the steps really fast – but not fast enough.

I heard a familiar laugh.

"DEAN!" I yelled. "DEAN, LET US OUT OF HERE."

"DON'T WORRY, BENJY," shouted my brother, "THE VAMPIRE WILL LET YOU OUT WHEN HE GETS BACK. YOU JUST HAVE TO WAIT TILL DAWN."

# Vampire Across the Way

We sat there till we couldn't hear Dean laughing any more.

"So now what?" asked Cas.

I forced myself to sound braver than I felt. "We're not waiting round here till dawn, that's for sure. Maybe we can get out the front door."

"But we can't see a thing," Cas objected.

"We'll just have to follow the wall."

"Right." Cas sighed. "You lead the way."

It was slow going.

"It's like walking through treacle," grumbled Cas.

It was more like walking through
a minefield. Every few
steps we'd bump
into something. The
first thing was a chair.

The second was a tea
chest. The third
wasn't either.

I moved the tiny
light back and forth.
It was a narrow pine box.

"Jeez…" Cas's voice sounded far away. "It really is a coffin."

I couldn't stop my hand from shaking. "D'you think we should look inside?"

"No." Cas sounded pretty certain. "I think we should get upstairs. Fast."

I didn't need any convincing.
Holding onto each other, we
charged through the darkness until
we ran into a door.

"I could kiss it," said Cas.

I took hold of the handle.

A tall, dark figure flew out at us.
We both screamed.

When I opened my eyes I could see that it was only a coat in a cupboard.

Finally we found the stairs that led to the ground floor.

"We're going to make it, Benjy! We're going to make it!"

"Of course we're going to make it." I said it like I'd never had any doubt. "Come on, let's get out of here."

We climbed up to the main hall. We could see the white of the front door at the end. It was only eight or nine metres away. Cas and I ran every millimetre.

"What if it's locked?" whispered Cas. "What if there's an alarm?"

"Well there's only one way to find out."

But before I could pull on the door, it suddenly opened by itself.

I jumped to get out of the way, fell into Cas, and we both landed on the floor.

I wasn't sure if I was more afraid that we were in the house of a vampire who was going to suck our blood or of a regular bloke who was going to tell my mother what we'd done. Either way I reckoned we were in big trouble.

"We can ex—"

The light went on.

The owner of the house was standing in the doorway, his hat pushed back on his head and his arms folded in front of him.

Both Cas and I knew who he was the second we saw him. His picture was always in the papers and he was always on the telly or smiling at you from a billboard or the back of a bus.

Together we said, "You're Bobby Boats!"

Bobby Boats said, "And who are you?"

Cas and I got to our feet.

"My name's Benjy, and this is my mate Cas. I live across the road."

Bobby Boats nodded. "And you're doing *what* in my house?"

I had nothing to lose by telling the truth.

"We're looking for vampires."

"You're looking for *what?*"

So I told him about seeing him move in. And about Dean locking us in the cellar.

He was very sympathetic. He had a big brother, too.

"Big brothers can get you into trouble," said Bobbie Boats.

I said, "Tell me about it."

# I finally Get a Photo to Hang Over my Desk

So my mum was right, there was no such thing as vampires. At least not in our neighbourhood.

What we had in our neighbourhood was a mega-famous pop star who was trying to get away from his fans for a while to write songs for his next album.

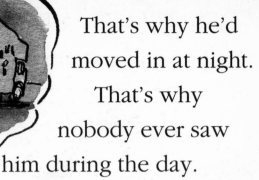
That's why he'd
moved in at night.
That's why
nobody ever saw
him during the day.
That's why he had
to sneak in and out
of his own home.
And what we'd
thought was a coffin was
the crate he packed his sound
equipment in.

Cas and I were sworn to secrecy.
"You mean we can't tell *anyone?*" asked Cas.

"No one," said Bobby Boats.

I frowned. "Not even my brother?"

"Especially not your brother."

Here was the best chance I'd ever had of getting one over on Dean and I couldn't take it. The disappointment must have shown on my face.

"I'll tell you what, though," said Bobby Boats. "If you promise not to tell anyone that I live here, I'll make sure you and your families get tickets for my next concert."

"Wow!" Cas was practically screeching. "That'd be brilliant!"

I wasn't totally thrilled. "Even my brother?" I didn't see why he should get a free ticket after what he'd done.

"Even your brother," said Bobby Boats. "Get him to bring his camera with him, so he can take a photo of you and me together."

And we did...

The photo of me and Cas and Bobby Boats still hangs over my desk.